HA!

that Leopard
fell out of
his tree.

He startled some bears,
who tripped on the stairs

# Hullabaloo
## at the Zoo

Zanna Davidson

Illustrated by
Alison Friend

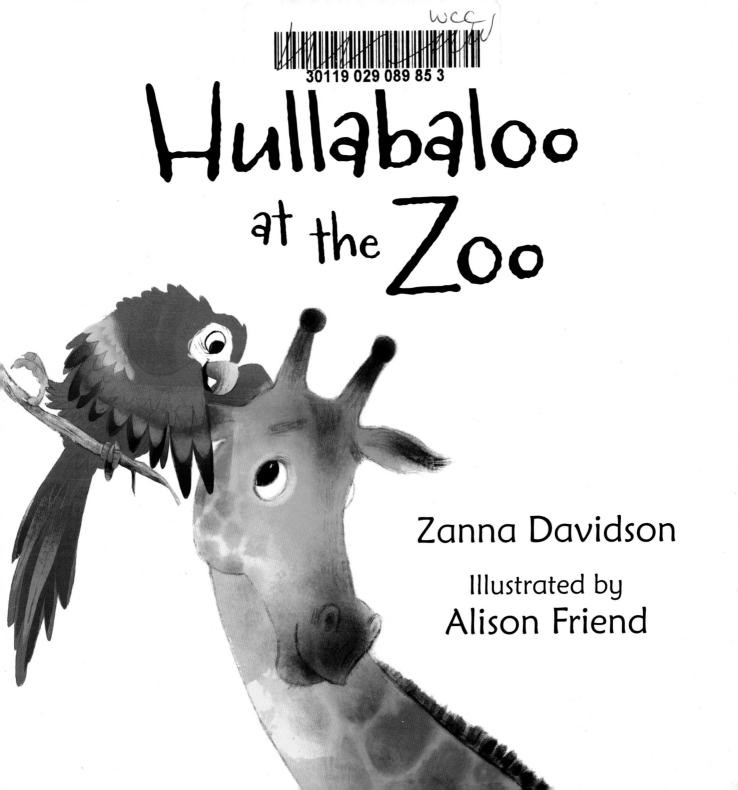

It began when Giraffe
gave such a GREAT laugh

HA

HA HA

and went **SPLAT** in the crocodiles' tea.

The crocs got a shock,

and ruined their frocks,
which came all the way
from Peru.

They jumped from their cages,
and went on RAMPAGES...

Bears

Lions

What a HULLABALOO at the ZOO!

The monkeys
were howling,

the owlets were scowling.

But Lion said,
"Let's have some
FUN!"

Into Africa

Then Zebra starts rapping,

soon everyone's clapping,

to the beat of the tortoise's drum.

The frilly-necked lizard
reveals he's a wizard
at playing the didgeridoo,

while the sloth
makes a din on his
new mandolin...

What a
HULLABALOO

The meerkats are bopping,
the lemurs are hopping.
Old Rhino is waltzing with flair.

She spins
into llamas...

...and **soaks** their pyjamas...

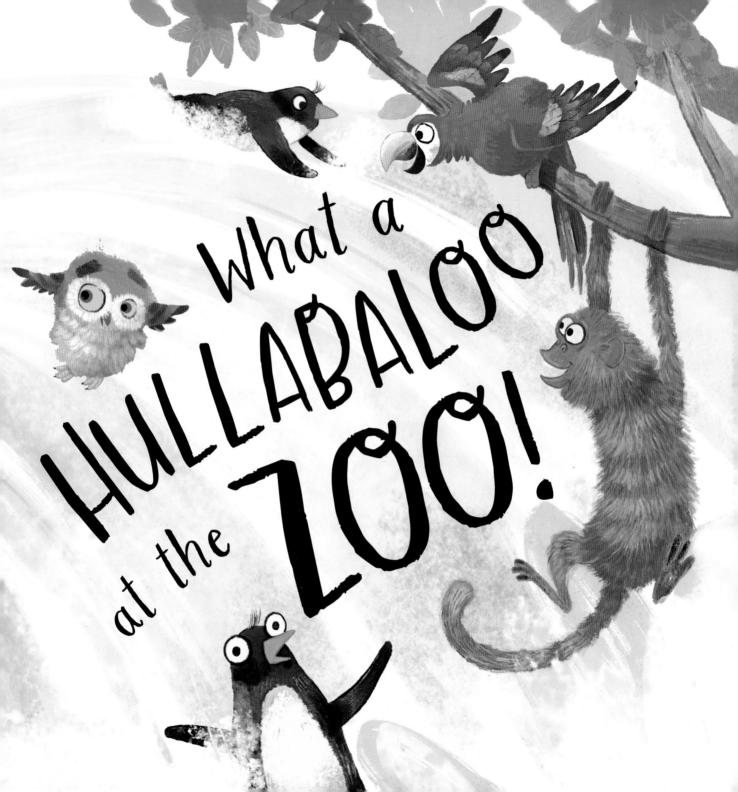

What a HULLABALOO at the ZOO!

"I'm tired," says Baboon,
bringing out his bassoon.
"I'll play something
calming and quiet."

His tune is so moving,
so peaceful and soothing,
it brings a swift end to the riot.

# The lions stop roaring.

The hippo is snoring
in the arms of the kangaroo.

And unless you had seen it,
you'd think you had dreamed it...

That HULLABALOO
at the ZOO!

Shhhh!

Penguins

Meerkats

Llamas

# About phonics

Phonics is a method of teaching reading which is used extensively in today's schools. At its heart is an emphasis on identifying the *sounds* of letters, or combinations of letters, that are then put together to make words. These sounds are known as phonemes.

## Starting to read

Learning to read is an important milestone for any child. The process can begin well before children start to learn letters and put them together to read words. The sooner children can discover books and enjoy stories and language, the better they will be prepared for reading themselves, first with the help of an adult and then independently.

You can find out more about phonics on the Usborne Very First Reading website, **usborne.com/veryfirstreading.** Click on the **Parents** tab at the top of the page, then scroll down and click on **About synthetic phonics**.

**Phonemic awareness**

An important early stage in pre-reading and early reading is developing phonemic awareness: that is, listening out for the sounds within words. Rhymes, rhyming stories and alliteration are excellent ways of encouraging phonemic awareness.

In this story, your child will soon identify the *oo* sound, as in **hullabaloo** and **zoo**. Look out, too, for rhymes such as **bears** – **stairs** and **bopping** – **hopping**.

**Hearing your child read**

If your child is reading a story to you, don't rush to correct mistakes, but be ready to prompt or guide if he or she is struggling. Above all, do give plenty of praise and encouragement.

Designed by Tabitha Blore
Edited by Jenny Tyler and Lesley Sims
Digital design by John Russell

Reading consultants: Alison Kelly
and Anne Washtell

First published in 2020 by Usborne Publishing Ltd., Usborne House,
83-85 Saffron Hill, London EC1N 8RT, England. usborne.com
Copyright © 2020 Usborne Publishing Ltd.